# Princess Tales

Retold by Jackie Andrews
Illustrated by Kate Davies

Award Publications Limited

# This book belongs to

..........................................

ISBN 978-1-84135-523-8

Cover illustration by Angela Hicks
Copyright © Award Publications Limited
Illustrations © 2006 Kate Davies

This edition first published 2007

Published by Award Publications Limited,
The Old Riding School, The Welbeck Estate,
Worksop, Nottinghamshire, S80 3LR

10 2

Printed in China

# Contents

# The Twelve
# Dancing Princesses

There was once a king who had twelve beautiful daughters.

They all shared one very large bedroom, and each night the king himself made sure they were safely locked in.

But when the king opened their door each morning he saw that their shoes had been worn to ribbons from dancing.

None of the princesses would explain how it happened.

So the king announced that whoever solved the
mystery would be given half the kingdom and
marry one of the princesses.

But if, after three nights, they tried to solve it
and failed, they would lose their lives.

It happened that a soldier heard of the king's challenge and decided he would try his luck. But on the way to the palace, he stopped to help an

old woman carry her heavy bundle of wood. She was very grateful.

When she heard that the soldier was going to try to solve the mystery of the dancing princesses, the old woman gave him a magic cloak that would make him invisible.

"And do not drink the wine the princesses will give you!" she warned him.

That night, the soldier settled himself outside the door to the princesses' bedroom. He only pretended

to drink the wine that the eldest princess gave him, and before long lay down as if he were fast asleep.

Then the eldest princess tapped on her bed, and it sank into the floor revealing a secret tunnel.

One by one they stepped down into it – and the clever soldier put on his magic cloak so he could not be seen and followed quietly behind them as they went out.

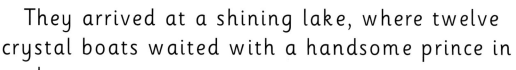

They arrived at a shining lake, where twelve crystal boats waited with a handsome prince in each.

The soldier stepped unseen into the boat of the youngest princess and in this way he saw the wonderful castle where the princesses danced with their princes until three o'clock in the morning.

After three nights, the king demanded to know what the soldier had discovered. The soldier told him all he had seen, and gave the king three

golden twigs he had taken from the branches of the trees near the castle the princesses visited every night.

The princesses were astounded when they heard they had been found out but had to admit that the soldier was right.

Their secret was discovered at last!

That same day, the soldier had his reward.

He married the king's eldest daughter, and was given half the kingdom, just as the king had promised.

# Cinderella

A long time ago there was a beautiful young girl who had a horrid stepmother and two unkind stepsisters.

Whenever she had finished the hard work they gave her, the girl sat in the cinders by the kitchen fire, where it was warm, and her two stepsisters called her Cinderella.

One day, an invitation arrived for a ball at the palace. The stepsisters set Cinderella to work immediately, helping them to get ready.

Once they had driven away to the palace, Cinderella sat down in the hearth and wished that she could go, too. She was very sad.

Then she heard a voice saying, "What is the matter, my dear?"

Cinderella looked up and saw a kindly old woman in front of her. "Who are you?" she asked, astonished.

The old woman smiled kindly at Cinderella and told her not to be afraid. "I am your fairy godmother," she said.

"I've come to help you go to the prince's ball, but you must do exactly what I tell you."

The old woman sent Cinderella to find a fat rat, six white mice, six green lizards, and the biggest pumpkin in the garden.

Then with a wave of her wand, the fairy godmother turned them into a golden coach with six horses, a coachman and six footmen.

With another wave of her wand she dressed Cinderella in a wonderful ball-gown and glass slippers.

"Off you go and enjoy yourself at the ball," said her fairy godmother, "but be sure to leave before midnight, when the magic will wear off!"

The prince noticed Cinderella as soon as she entered the ballroom, because she looked so beautiful. He danced with her the whole night.

The two stepsisters were jealous but did not recognise the mysterious princess at all.

Cinderella enjoyed herself so much at the ball that she forgot all about the time until she heard the clock begin to strike twelve!

Then Cinderella suddenly remembered what her kind fairy godmother had said to her and ran from the ballroom. As she ran out of the palace she dropped one of her glass slippers.

The prince picked it up and said he would only marry the lady that the slipper fitted.

A royal herald went round the land trying the slipper on all the unmarried ladies, but it fitted none of them.

When the royal herald, who was really the prince in disguise, came to Cinderella's house both the stepsisters tried on the glass slipper. But it did not fit either of them.

When he saw Cinderella the royal herald insisted that she also should try on the slipper, which made the unkind stepsisters laugh.

But shyly, Cinderella came forward and, of course, the slipper fitted her perfectly. Immediately her ragged gown changed into a beautiful dress.

The prince threw off his disguise and took Cinderella to his palace where they were married the very next day.

# Beauty and the Beast

A merchant, who had once been rich, had lost a fortune when his ship sank at sea. One day he had to go away on business and he asked his children what presents they would like him to bring back from the city.

The older children wanted expensive things, but his youngest daughter, Beauty, asked for a single rose.

On his way home, the merchant suddenly found himself in a wonderful garden. He saw a rose bush covered in blooms and picked one for Beauty.

"Surely it won't matter if I just take one," he thought. But suddenly a horrible beast appeared, terrifying the merchant.

"Why are you stealing my roses?" roared the Beast. "I will kill you for that!"

The merchant begged the Beast to forgive him, and explained the rose was a gift for his youngest daughter.

36

"Very well," said the Beast. "I will spare your life, but only if one of your daughters will come and live with me here."

The merchant went home feeling very sad. How could he ask one of his children to live with such a monster?

But Beauty was not afraid to go. "I will stay with the Beast, Father. It was my fault this happened," she said.

With a heavy heart the merchant took her to the Beast's castle and left her there.

Beauty lived like a queen at the Beast's castle.
But every day, as she sat down to supper with the
Beast, he asked her a terrible question:

"Will you marry me, Beauty?" And she was too
afraid to reply.

One day, Beauty asked the Beast to let her visit her family. He told her she must promise to come back in two months or he would die.

He also gave her food and several chests of treasure to take home with her, and waved her goodbye.

The two months went by quickly without Beauty noticing; she was so pleased to be with her family.

Then one night she dreamed of the Beast. He was dying. Beauty went straight back to the castle, using a magic ring the Beast had given her, but she could not find him anywhere.

Beauty ran into the garden and by the light of
the moon found the Beast lying on the grass. He
was very ill.

"Oh, Beast, don't die!" cried Beauty. "I didn't
realise how much I loved you. Please forgive me."

"Beauty!" whispered the Beast, slowly opening his eyes and looking up at her. "You're back! Will you marry me now?"

"Yes!" she said. "I will marry you."
And then, with a great flash of light and loud music, the Beast disappeared...

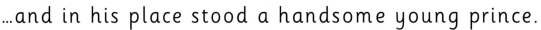

...and in his place stood a handsome young prince.

"By agreeing to be my wife," he told her, "you have broken a terrible spell that a wicked witch put upon me."

And so Beauty and the Beast became a prince and princess and were very happy.

# Rumpelstiltskin

In a land far away, a poor miller went to see the king one day. The miller had a plan to make himself rich.

"My lovely daughter," he told the king, "can spin straw into real gold!"

Now the king was very fond of gold, so he asked the miller to bring his daughter to the palace the very next day, so he could see the miracle for himself.

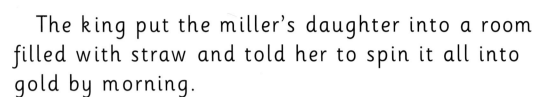

The king put the miller's daughter into a room filled with straw and told her to spin it all into gold by morning.

"If you don't," said the king, "your father will be killed."

She did not know what to do. How could she possibly spin straw into gold?

"Oh, if only there was someone who could help me with this impossible task!" she wept.

Suddenly, a door opened. A funny little man came into the room and asked her why she was so sad.

The miller's daughter told him her story.

"What will you give me if I spin all this straw into gold for you?" asked the little man.

"My necklace," the girl replied.

The little man took the necklace, and then sat down at the spinning-wheel. By morning the room was full of gold.

The king could hardly believe his eyes when he saw it.

He took the girl into an even larger room filled with straw that he wanted spun into gold as well. "Finish it by morning if you want to see your father again!" he told her.

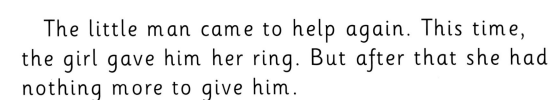

The little man came to help again. This time, the girl gave him her ring. But after that she had nothing more to give him.

So when the king put her into an even bigger room filled with yet more straw, the little man asked a terrible price for his help.

"Promise to give me your first-born child when you are queen," said the little man. The miller's daughter thought that she would never be a queen, so she agreed.

The straw was spun into gold once more and in the morning the king was so pleased, he made the miller's daughter his queen.

When the queen's baby was born, the little man came again – this time to collect his promised fee. The queen was distraught as she loved her baby dearly.

"Very well," said the little man. "I'll give you three days to find out my name. After that, the baby is mine!"

Immediately, the king sent a servant to find out the little man's name. But of all the strange names he discovered, none was the right one.

Then on the third day, he came across a funny little man singing: "Rumpelstiltskin is my name!"
The servant rushed back to the palace with his news.

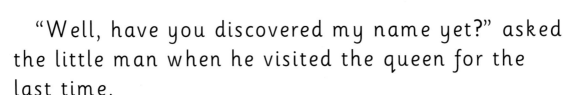

"Well, have you discovered my name yet?" asked the little man when he visited the queen for the last time.

The queen pretended to be uncertain. "Is your name… Rumpelstiltskin?" she asked.

The little man was very cross. "A witch has told you!" he shrieked, stamping his feet angrily. But finally he left the palace and was never seen again.

# The Princess
# and the Pea

There was once a prince who wanted a wife. But he only wanted to marry a real princess.

So he left the palace and set off to find one. He soon discovered that this was not going to be easy.

He met a great many royal ladies, but couldn't be sure if they were really, truly princesses.

Besides, there was always something wrong with them; they were too short, too tall, too thin, too fat, too stupid or too vain. The prince returned home, very sad and disappointed.

One night, there was a very bad storm that shook the palace and lit up the sky with lightning.

Someone knocked on the palace door, and the king himself went to open it.

It was a girl! She told the king she was a princess and asked if she could shelter from the storm.

It was hard to tell what she was, her clothes were soaked, her hair dripped and she was blue with cold. But the king kindly asked her to come inside out of the rain, wondering if this could be the real princess his son was looking for.

The queen, however, wasn't convinced. But she knew how to tell if the princess was a real one or not.

She ordered a special bed to be made up for the visitor.

It was piled high with twenty mattresses, one on top of the other, and then twenty blankets on top of them.

Under all these, the queen secretly put a single dried pea.

The queen took the princess to her room. The princess climbed up on to the strange bed using a stepladder.

Then the queen wished her a good night and pleasant dreams and the princess tried to get some sleep.

She tossed and turned, this way and that, trying to get comfortable, but something kept digging into her, keeping her awake.

In the morning she felt tired and bruised.

When the royal family met for breakfast next morning, the queen asked the princess if she had slept well.

"Not at all!" replied the princess. "I was very uncomfortable. There was something hard in the bed that dug into me all night. I just couldn't find out what it was. I'm black and blue all over."

The queen was very pleased. She knew that only a real princess would have felt the pea under all

those mattresses. She decided that she would tell the king once he had finished his breakfast.

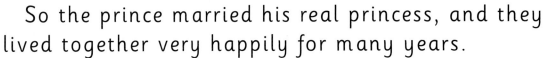

So the prince married his real princess, and they lived together very happily for many years.

The pea was put into a glass case and was kept in the royal museum. And there it has stayed to this very day.

# The Sleeping Beauty

Once upon a time, a great many important people and fairies were invited to the christening of a baby princess.

The king and queen had waited many years for their first child and they were very happy that at last their daughter had been born.

Unfortunately there was one fairy who wasn't invited but who came anyway. She was a spiteful old fairy.

While everyone else gave good gifts to the baby she promised that one day the princess would prick her finger on a spindle and die.

The youngest fairy came forward. "I cannot undo the spell the old woman has put upon her," she told the king and queen. "But I can tell you the princess will not die."

She waved her wand over the sleeping baby and said, "Instead she will sleep for a hundred years, until a king's son wakes her with a kiss."

From that day on all spinning-wheels and
spindles were destroyed and forbidden.

The little princess was watched carefully, and
grew up to be a beautiful and happy child.

Then one day, when she was exploring the attic in the palace, the princess came across an old woman working at a spinning-wheel.

It was the wicked fairy in disguise!
The princess was fascinated as she had never seen a spinning-wheel before and she wanted to try it for herself.

But as she reached for the spindle, it pricked her finger and immediately she fell down in a deep, deep sleep.

It was just as the youngest fairy had promised.

Nothing the king and queen tried would wake her. So they laid the princess gently on her bed, kissed her and left.

Then the youngest fairy put a spell on the palace so that everything in it would sleep until the princess woke up.

The palace immediately became covered with brambles and thorns, hiding it completely except for the highest turrets.

It became a place of mystery and in time it was forgotten except for the stories mothers told to their children.

A hundred years went by. One day a prince came to hunt in the woods round the palace and saw the turrets peeping above the trees.

Remembering the old tales his nurse had told him, he hacked his way through the brambles with his sword to look for the sleeping princess.

He went through all the rooms, past sleeping animals and people, until he found a beautiful maiden asleep on a golden bed.

The prince kissed her forehead, and immediately the princess opened her eyes and smiled, and the palace came awake again.

The prince and the princess were married that night, with feasting, dancing and music.

They lived very happily together, for the rest of their lives.

# The Princess
# and the Frog

One summer evening a young princess was playing with her golden ball in the palace garden.

She threw the ball too high and it bounced far away from her, fell into the pond and sank out of sight.

The princess looked into the pond, but couldn't see anything: it was too deep and dark.

She began to cry. "I would give anything to have my beautiful ball back," she sobbed. "Anything in the world."

83

Just then a frog popped up out of the water.
"Why are you crying?" he asked the princess.

The princess told him, "My ball has fallen into
this pond, and I can't reach it by myself."

"I will bring back your ball," said the frog, "as long as you promise to let me come and live with

you in the castle, eat off your plate and sleep on your bed at night. And you must love me."

Now the princess had no intention of letting the frog come home with her. And she certainly could never love him! But she wanted her ball back.

"Very well," she said, "I promise. If you bring me back my ball I will do everything you ask."
The frog dived into the water.

After a little while, the frog popped up again with the ball in his mouth. He dropped the ball at her feet.

Overjoyed, the princess quickly picked the ball up and ran home, completely forgetting her promise to the frog.

The next day, just as the princess and her family had sat down to dinner, there was a knock on the palace door.

The princess opened the door, and there was the frog on the doorstep. She shut the door quickly and ran back to the table, very white and shaken.

"What has upset you?" asked the king.

The princess told her father about losing her golden ball. "And now the horrid frog is at the door and wants to come in!" she said.

As soon as the king heard what had happened, he told the princess she must keep her promise. "Go and let him in!" he commanded.

So, for three days and nights, the princess had to let the frog sit at the table with her and sleep on her pillow at night.

Each time the princess thought she had got rid of the horrible frog, he came back to remind her of her promise.

But the next morning, she had a big surprise.
By her bed stood a handsome young prince!

He explained that an evil fairy had turned him
into a frog, but the princess had broken the spell by
being kind to him.

The prince took the princess back to his father's

kingdom where they were married and lived
happily together for many years.